Plankton Is PUSHY

To Tom and Shirley, with a son's love.

ISBN: 978-1-338-15886-1
10 9 8 7 6 5 4 3 2 1   17 18 19 20 21

Printed in the U.S.A. 08
First printing 2017

Book design by Steve Ponzo

Plankton Is PUSHY

Jonathan Fenske

Scholastic Inc.

SNAP!

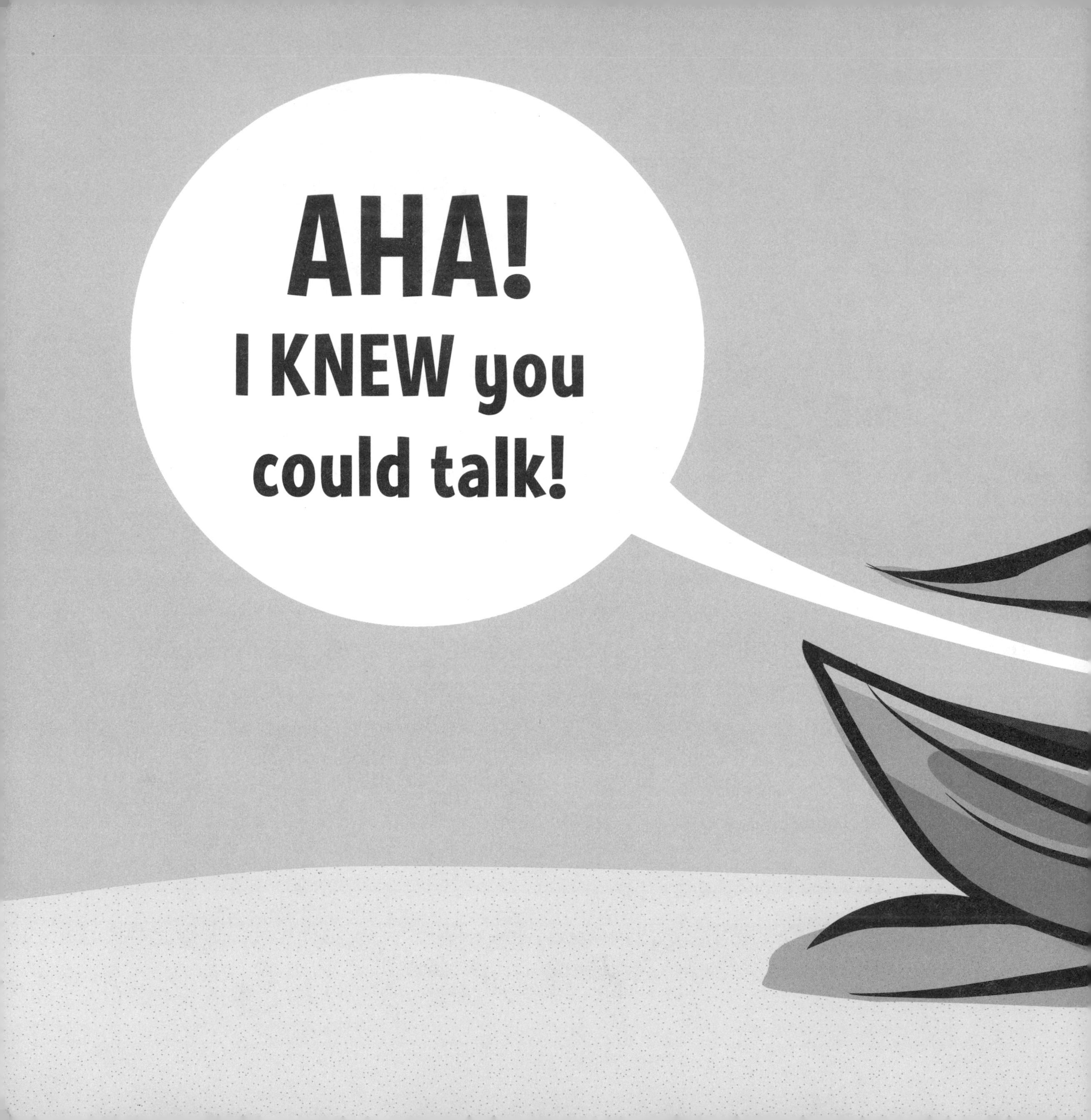
AHA!
I KNEW you could talk!